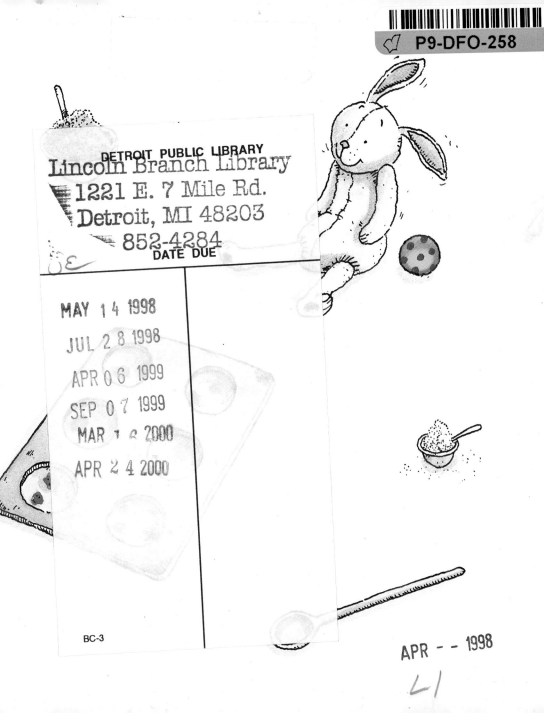

Edited by Anna McQuinn and Ambreen Husain
Designed by Suzy McGrath and Sarah Godwin

First published in the United States in 1996 by
De Agostini Editions Ltd, 919 Third Avenue,
New York, NY 10022

Distributed by Stewart, Tabori & Chang
a division of U.S. Media Holdings, Inc.,
New York, NY

ISBN 1-899883-63-0
Library of Congress Catalog Card Number:
96-83838

Printed and bound in Italy

Food Science Consultant
Shirley Corriher

For Baby Splib, CF
For Brenda, HR

My Sister is SUPER!

Illustrated by
Chris Fisher

Written by
Hannah Roche

My sister is super!

Today she took out some little
paper cups and put them in
a muffin pan.

She said this was a good trick
to keep the surprise from sticking.

Then she put some flour, sugar, baking powder and salt in a bowl and told me to mix them up.

She says it's the baking powder
that works the magic.

Next she mixed an egg, some milk and oil in another bowl.

Then we poured her eggy mixture
into my dry one and mixed them
together until they were gooey.

Finally we got some raspberries
and put them in as well.

(Well, not all of them –
I had to check one
or two to make sure
they were fresh.)

We spooned all the mixture into
the paper cups – but Sophie said
not to fill them up to the top.

Then she put them in the oven.

"Don't touch the oven," she said,
"but if you watch,
you will see the
magic happening."

I did see the magic – the mixture got bigger and bigger and came right up above the top of the little paper cups!

Abracadabra!

They had turned into **muffins!**

They were lovely and spongy
and red right through!

Yum!

I love
my super
sister!

Notes for Parents

EVEN very young children are aware that water is wet, rock is hard, sand is grainy. As they observe more, children discover that things don't always stay the same – whipping, heating, mixing, freezing and so on make things change from gooey to spongy, from soft to hard, from liquid to solid....

LEARNING to notice and describe the textures and changes is important to children's understanding of the world around them. Don't worry about using "proper" scientific words – getting the description right is what really matters.

YOU can recreate the story in your own kitchen by following the recipe opposite. As you go along, encourage your child to talk about what's happening. Then, you can eat the results!

HOW IT WORKS

ACIDS and bases chemically react together in the presence of moisture or heat and produce carbon dioxide bubbles. Baking powder contains acid and a base (baking soda) and you can see them react if you put a spoon of baking powder into water.

WHEN you bake, the carbon dioxide bubbles swell inside the batter and stretch it – this makes the batter rise.

MOST baking powder is double-acting – it is called double-acting because it first works when you mix it with the moist ingredients and then again during the heat of baking when you cook it.

Michael's Recipe

YOU WILL NEED:

2 cups of all-purpose flour

¼ cup of sugar

2 teaspoons of double-acting
baking powder

¼ teaspoon of salt

1 egg

1 cup of milk

¼ cup of vegetable oil

1 cup of raspberries

bowls, muffin pans, paper baking
cups (optional), a tablespoon,
teaspoons, wooden spoons and
a wire rack

HINTS

BE CAREFUL not to overfill the paper
cups. Filling them just two-thirds full
allows the batter to rise during baking
without spilling over the edges.

1. Turn on your oven to 400°F/200°C.
2. Put the paper cups in the muffin pans,
   or grease the pans with butter.
3. In one bowl, mix together the flour,
   sugar, baking powder and salt.
4. In another bowl, mix the egg, milk
   and vegetable oil.
5. Add the milk mixture to the dry ingredients
   and stir with a wooden spoon just until all
   the dry ingredients are moistened.
6. Add the raspberries and mix gently.
7. Using a large spoon, fill each paper cup
   two-thirds full of batter.
8. Bake for 20 to 25 minutes, then remove
   from the oven and place on a wire rack.
   Allow to cool for about five minutes.